A First-Start Easy Reader

This easy reader contains only 61 different words,
repeated often to help the young reader develop
word recognition and interest in reading.

Basic word list for *Susie Goes Shopping*

did	an	is
not	can	Susie
her	day	Susie's
you	feel	mother
go	well	bakery
to	said	dollar
the	will	dollars
for	have	please
me	loaf	bread
she	then	walked
do	saw	asked
I	cake	large
one	make	frosted
six	pie	better
buy	good	apple
a	baker	dozen
of	only	cookies
at	home	cannot
so	thank	want
gave	this	what
	just	

Susie
Goes Shopping

Written by Rose Greydanus

Illustrated by Margot Apple

Troll Associates

One day, Susie's mother

did not feel well.

"Susie," said her mother.

"Will you go to the bakery for me?"

"I do not feel well."

Her mother gave her one dollar.

Bread

"Please buy a loaf of bread
at the bakery."

Susie walked to the bakery.

She asked for a loaf of bread.

Then she saw a large, frosted cake.

M-m-m, good.

"A large, frosted cake will make
Mother feel better."

So Susie asked for the
large, frosted cake.

Then she saw an apple pie. M-m-m, good.

"An apple pie will make Mother feel better."

So Susie asked for the apple pie.

Then she saw a dozen cookies.

M-m-m, good.

"A dozen cookies will make

Mother feel better."

So Susie asked for a dozen cookies.

The baker said, "Six dollars, please."

Susie did not have six dollars.

"I cannot buy the large, frosted cake,"
said Susie.

"I cannot buy the dozen cookies."

"I cannot buy the apple pie."

"I can only buy the loaf of bread."

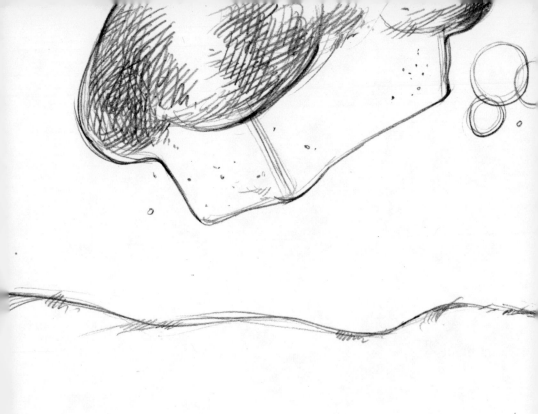

Then Susie walked home.

She gave her mother

the loaf of bread.

"Thank you," said her mother.

"This is just what I want."

"M-m-m, good."